Root

A NOVELLA

— • —

LLOYD MATTHEW THOMPSON

STARFIELD

ROOT
by Lloyd Matthew Thompson
Copyright © 2013 Starfield Press
www.StarfieldPress.com

First printing 2013
Second printing 2020

Paperback ISBN: 978-0615851198

This book is a work of fiction. Names, characters, places, and incidents are purely of the author's imagination. Any resemblance to actual events, locales, or persons living or dead, is entirely coincidental.

Cover art: *The Lament for Icarus*
by Herbert James Draper, 1898

Cover design by Lloyd Matthew Thompson

A NOVELLA

— • —

LLOYD MATTHEW THOMPSON

He didn't remember exactly where he was before he had a body, but he definitely remembered where he was when he became aware he was now *inside* a body.

The harder he tried to remember *before*, though, the further it seemed to slip away. He had to have known at one time— he remembers there *was* a "one time," doesn't he? Why was it now cruelly held captive at the edge of his awareness, taunting and teasing his muffled soul?

His awareness. That's another thing he now found frustrating, though he cannot quite explain why, if asked.

Before, there were no limitations on his awareness. Had there been any restrictions then? It seems there used to be a time when he was not so *confined* in his senses. Things were different then— weren't they? It's so difficult to tell now.

One thing he did know: he did not belong here. He was not from this place, he was not made for this place, he did not belong in this place.

He was sure of it.

But to this place he had come.

His first awareness came from above. He was in a tree, clinging for dear life to the highest, thinnest branch that would support his weight without snapping and sending him tumbling into the hands of the angry throng below.

Dear life? He supposed life was dear, even if it was not his own life. But this *was* his life, wasn't it? Had it always been? No, there had been *something* else, before. Yet he reacted as if this *was* his own life, in this moment.

Looking down on the crowd screaming for him sent waves of tense electricity through his body. His every muscle seemed to tighten around the slender branch more than should have been possible for this body. Had this always been his body? He thinks it has been. And these Others with their twisted faces and boiling eyes wanted him to come down, wanted him to do something, wanted to do something *to* him!

A new shock went through his system, and shivers began tormenting his body uncontrollably. What *was* this sensation? He looked to the sky as a wetness filled his eyes. The brightness on the large cloud drifting by blurred into the sparkling of jewels overhead. A darkened speck moving across the glare grew larger, came closer, took shape. It was an animal, flying. *Bird,* his mind named it as it appeared to be coming to rest in his tree, then changed its mind and veered away at the last second. The wetness rolled down his cheek as his body continued to shake. *Tears. Crying.* Crying because the bird flew away, or because he was stuck in a tree? Stuck in a tree, or being chased by a mob?

Tremors that were not from his body entered his awareness. A cry escaped him, the sound of his own voice startling as he looked down to find his tree was now being hit by two separate men in the crowd. Swinging heavy sticks with sharp metal attached, they took turns chopping into what little sense of safety he had.

Panic gripped his body at a new level. What were they going to do to him? *Why* were they doing this? What was going to happen? What would become of his body? How was he going to get away? He needed this body— his body! What would he do if he lost it? What would become of *him?*

The cracking of wood accompanied a disorientation in his awareness. The limb began moving, though his own limbs did not. His tree tumbled over, its roots left behind.

And Lam fell to earth.

• TWO •

Pressing his hand to the tree for support, Lam doubled over and gasped for air. His heart was unaware his legs had stopped running, and continued to run in circles within its cage of ribs. The blood pounded in his ears so loudly he was sure his pursuers would be able to hear it, and find him again.

The crowd had forgotten their anger long enough to split frantically and avoid being crushed by his falling tree. Lam had landed hard, flat on his back. It had knocked the wind from his lungs, but he'd recovered quickly and scrambled into a run as the gap between him and the Others swiftly closed. He hadn't even had to think about it. It was as if his body had a mind of its own— it just got up and ran.

He had lost the Others twice in his flight, and been discovered twice. Only after ducking into a feeble structure, out its back entrance, scratching through the shadows of a thicket, and splashing through a stream did he slow down enough to realize he had lost them for good. For now.

He glanced back, making sure once more the Others were not in sight. His panting was beginning to subside, his mind beginning to clear. He glanced up into this new tree. It had droopy leaves instead of the tall, uplifted branches the one he had fallen from had had. Should he climb its branches and return to where he felt safe? Was that where he belonged? The vivid memory of his recent fall returned and quickly pursued the associations of safety and heights, replacing it with the opposite.

His heart sent another surge of electricity through his system, and he backed away as if this tree, too, would fall on him at any second.

Tripping on a stone, he fell backwards into a cluster of fuzzy vine-like plants. Grateful it was not the brambles that had torn and bitten his skin as he had clawed his way through in desperation to reach this place, he sighed and felt his body relax, if only slightly. There were no Others to be seen here. No sounds but those of the trees and plants stirring in the breeze. He was alone, the only one in this place, abandoned in an unknown land, rejected, cut off from his home. He had nowhere he belonged.

Home? Was *that* the "before?" If so, where *was* this home? Where was he supposed to go? What was he supposed to be doing? He had been doing something, hadn't he? He felt sure of it. But what?

His eyes drifted to the sky once again, and found even the clouds had abandoned him. Lam thought of the bird that had almost joined him. Why had it changed its mind? Had it rejected him, or rejected the mob below him? Where had it flown instead? Where were *any* of the animals here? It was extremely quiet. He missed the constant chatter in his head. It felt so empty without it, so lonely. Had it been noisier at *home*, or was it merely the absence of the angry crowd screaming for his life that now rang in his ears? There was no way for him to know. It was all so confusing, all so hopeless.

Lam sighed and allowed his body to release more of its tension. It really did feel wonderful to loosen his muscles. They were so heavy. His entire body felt so bulky, so weak. He wasn't used to this. Lying on the soft bed of vines and gazing into the expanse of sky spread above him brought feelings of peace and relaxation within him. Something about the sky stirred *something* in his body. It was a wash of electricity through his system, like that of the fear when he was running, but somehow different.

Ah, *fear*. That's what that had been. That sounded right. Then what was this new feeling?

He didn't know why the sky was blue here, but its shade began darkening, then returned to its full brightness, only to be dimmed to an even darker hue. The brightness returned as he inhaled a deep breath of air into his lungs and opened his drooping eyes fully once more.

He exhaled the air as he drifted into blackness and dreams of things he could no longer remember.

• THREE •

A sharp stick jabbed his ribs. He screamed and tried to leap up. He needed to run again— the Others had found him! He had to protect his body!

But his body would not respond. It would not rise *or* run.

The huge round face of an old woman filled his vision. Her large round eyes mirrored the shape of her face. Their hazel color appeared to be so light they looked yellow, and flickered as her toothless mouth spread into a grin. A rank odor flooded his nostrils as she chuckled and inspected his face. Lam struggled again as the old woman leaned in even closer, her long beak of a nose nearly touching his. The only way she would have been able to achieve this angle of examination was if she were sitting on him. He realized she was, and fear coursed through his veins once again. What was she going to do to him? He thrashed his body as hard as he could, trying to buck her off.

The woman's wrinkled fingers touched the center of his forehead, instantly calming him. Her hand grabbed both sides of his jaw firmly, and turned his head to one side. Tilting her own head slightly upward, she peered down her nose at him. A wet clucking sound came from her mouth as she turned him the other way. "Hmmm…" she muttered, releasing his face and sitting up straight on him.

Lam now saw the sky had grown dark, as if the blackness that had overtaken his vision in sleep had somehow stained the expanse, and he had ruined it forever. Maybe that's why the old woman had pinned him to the ground. Why wasn't he afraid anymore?

In the light of a huge bonfire raging nearby, he saw he was no longer where he had fallen asleep. Gone were the droopy leaves hanging over him, and the soft bed of vines underneath him. How had he gotten here? The flames from the fire, with its sparks and embers floating into the night, mesmerized him. Had he ever seen anything so beautiful? The sky had been beautiful, but had it been as beautiful as this fire? He realized this was the flicker reflecting in the old woman's eyes, and almost smiled as the thought occurred to him that this same beauty was flickering in his own eyes as well.

Beyond the sound of the round woman's labored breathing, Lam became aware he was hearing something else. Consistent chirping came from the darkness in all directions. Had the birds returned? Had they been waiting for night to come out? That seemed odd. No, this must be something else. Weren't there night creatures here? *Crickets.* Yes. The silence that had deafened him was broken at last, by crickets. Lam did smile now. He was no longer alone.

"SEED!"

The old woman jolted him from his thoughts. How was such an old woman able to project her voice so *loudly?*

A murmuring joined in the chorus of crickets. Voices! There were people here! Had the Others found him after all? Was this woman one of them? His internal anxiety increased, but his body remained strangely calm and unmoving. He knew his life was over now. His body was already lost.

With the aid of a thick tree branch that had been stripped and shaped, the woman slowly stood her plump, old body off him. He realized that was most likely the stick that had been used to poke him awake.

She spread her arms to each side, never taking her eyes from his face, never dropping the smile from her face. There was a rustling and shuffling all around, and Lam saw a ring of people moving into view. They drew closer and stared at him. Lam squeezed his eyes shut and felt the tension in his body increase as he braced for the Others to recognize him and rush to attack him.

"Ric'ua!" the old woman called out. The Others did not attack him, but instead gathered tighter and seemed to be even more interested in him than before. What had she told them? Were these not the Others? A woman broke from the circle around him. Her figure was silhouetted against the bonfire as she cautiously approached them. She moved to the other side of them and knelt to the earth. The blaze now illuminated her features. Her eyes sparkled and glowed as if they were made of diamonds. The fire accented what lines and wrinkles life had given her, but it was difficult to determine her age. She stared at Lam for a brief moment before turning her face up to the standing woman.

"Your son no longer lives," the round one said.

A wail burst from the woman kneeling beside him. The diamond sparkles in her eyes fell to her cheeks and rushed to her chin. She collapsed to the ground, moaning and shuddering. Gasps and cries rose from the crowd all around. The old woman raised her arms to the people, signaling for silence.

"Ric'ua," she spoke to the weeping woman, "Ric'ua, mourn as you must, but you are blessed this night." Ric'ua raised her head to look at her. Streaks of mud caked her face, a mask of dirt and tears.

"But, Shen-Ma… my *child*..." She trailed into sobs once again. Lam looked in wonder from woman to woman.

The old one hobbled the few steps it took to lay her hand on Ric'ua's head. "Your child has willingly stepped aside. He has seen the great need of this land, and offered himself in service, that a Seed may be planted in his place."

"He was only sent for gurja fruit!" Ric'ua howled, oblivious to the eyes resting on her every move, the ears hanging on her every word. "He was to return quickly! My son was told!"

The Shen-Ma patted her head gently. "This is your son now."

"NO!" she screeched. "I will not have it! I won't! I will have my Pael! This is *not* my son!" The crowd stood motionless, barely breathing, neither moving to assist, nor in a hurry to comfort the distraught member of their own. It was as if they knew they must not interfere with this interaction. Were they afraid? If they were afraid, which were they afraid of— the old woman or the mother?

"This *is* your son."

"No! He is different. This is *not* Pael!"

"No," agreed the old woman, "This is the body of Pael, but this is not Pael. You have been gifted Another.

"Before you now is the Seed of the Stars."

The people collectively gasped as understanding suddenly ran rampant among them. The Shen-Ma's words were repeated and whispered from person to person. They snuck uncomfortable glances at him as they stepped back, their circle expanding once again. Their bodies and curiosity retreated deeper into the shadows.

From the ground, another understanding also dawned. They were not afraid of the women.

They were afraid of Lam.

• FOUR •

"What is your name?"

Ric'ua scurried back a few paces, as if nearness to him would become dangerous when he spoke. The Shen-Ma shifted her great round belly toward him, to further indicate he had been addressed. "What are you called?"

He looked from the Shen-Ma to the mother. Her mud mask was quickly drying and cracking, giving her face a reptilian appearance. Her breathing was quick and shallow. Her shoulders visibly shook. He knew she could burst into tears again at any moment, and he did not wish that for her. Something within him felt *warm* towards her.

The tree branch prodded his ribs again. He turned back to the Shen-Ma, who simply waited patiently.

"L-Lam," he said.

"Lam," she repeated. She spread her arms again to the ring of people. "He is called Lam!" she bellowed. "Pael is no longer among us, but we have been gifted with Lam!

"He is The Seed!"

The crowd burst into cheers and shouts of

rejoicing. They moved in closer, dancing and clapping, quickly abandoning their circle formation. The Shen-Ma extended a hand to Lam, and he found his body would now respond. He grasped her strong hand and allowed her to pull him to his feet. The people formed themselves into a single audience before the three of them as the Shen-Ma offered her other hand to Ric'ua. The woman hesitated, and seemed to notice the crowd for the first time, though she had come from it herself. She stared at the people, wide-eyed.

"Ric'ua," the Shen-Ma beckoned. Ric'ua slowly stood and took her hand. The old woman smiled reassuringly and nodded. She pulled Lam and Ric'ua's hands together before the bonfire. The people held their breath, watching their fingers interlace as the Shen-Ma wished. The old woman raised their joined hands as high as her thick arms could reach.

"The Mother and The Son!" she cried.

The crowd erupted into joyful shouts once again as the old woman leaned close to the two before her. "Take him home now, Ric'ua. Embrace your son."

Ric'ua appeared momentarily horrified, as if it hadn't yet occurred on her that she would be bringing him home. Lam felt a similar hesitation, but the warmth and familiarity that was also inside him for this woman quickly overcame it. He wasn't sure what had happened to him, but he realized he did want to go with Ric'ua. He smiled at her and offered his other hand. Seemingly comforted by his gesture, she slowly placed her hand inside it. With their eyes locked on each other's, they stood together as their own circle in front of the Shen-Ma, in front of the bonfire, in front of the people, in front of the stars.

The old woman had said he was of the stars. What

was the word she had used? Seed. He knew seeds were planted. Had the stars planted him? Were there people among the stars? If so, why had they planted him here? These people here seemed to know him already though. Had he been planted some time ago, and it was just now being recognized? Why didn't he remember?

He knew seeds grew into plants, and he knew that after a time, plants bore fruit. This could explain why it was just now becoming known. Perhaps his fruit was just beginning to show.

Another part of him also knew fruit was then plucked.

Yet Lam felt he knew this woman. He was aware that Ric'ua was the most familiar to him of all these people. The warmth for her in his chest spread to his face, and his smile widened naturally and easily. What was this feeling? There was a word for it. *Love.* Yes, he thought. Love. Comfort. Safety. He felt safe with this woman. He wanted to be near this woman.

The crowd continued to celebrate as Ric'ua— now bearing a tiny but cautious smile of her own— released his second hand and turned to the side. She began leading Lam away from the fire, away from the people.

The old woman suddenly released an ear-piercing cry. Lam whipped his head around to see both her arms up, raising her stick to the skies. Ric'ua seemed to pay no attention, and continued walking, beginning to pull Lam along a bit roughly, like a mother with her grips on a child who has misbehaved.

They crossed back over the stream he had splashed through as he fled the Others. A fear began to creep into his mind again. Were these the Others after all?

Was she leading him right back to where he would be caught and killed? No, he could not go here! He didn't want to die!

Just as the urge to break free of her grasp and run again reached a peak, they came to the cluster of dwellings he had also passed. Ric'ua turned toward a hut next to the largest tree in the area, and led him inside. A new level of familiarity descended upon him. He had been here before. In that moment, Lam realized he had not fully believed these people. Even the warm and *knowing* feelings he felt with Ric'ua had not fully convinced him. He had still assumed it was all a case of mistaken identity, and could be humored until it was safe to do otherwise. It could all be sorted out later— anything to keep himself from being killed.

"What happened to me?" he asked.

Ric'ua turned and looked at him quickly, but said nothing. She pointed to a pallet of straw and furs in one corner of the room.

Lam was confused. Hadn't she heard him? Did she have no intention of talking to him? Why had she brought him here? Was she afraid of the Shen-Ma, and therefore doing only as the old woman asked, and no more?

"But I don't understand…" he trailed off as Ric'ua merely jabbed her finger at the corner. He slowly went and laid down. He became aware he *was* exhausted again, and found himself drifting to sleep, despite his better judgment— he still had no confirmation he was truly safe here yet.

FIVE

Ric'ua barely acknowledged Lam for three days.

Each day, he wandered out of the house and into the village, pretending not to notice the stares and whispers of those around him. The tension was nearly thick enough to cut with a knife, but he sensed no actual hostility toward him. By the end of the third day, he had relaxed enough— or gotten used to it enough— that he barely noticed. Or perhaps it was the people who had grown used to him, though none would speak of what had happened to him.

He stumbled across a large field hidden in a grove of trees on the second day. A dozen of the people were scattered throughout the field, on their hands and knees, intently and carefully yanking weeds from crops. Lam watched them closely until he was sure which plants they were pulling, and which they were leaving. He went to an empty space and began inspecting it for the weeds. It felt good to have his hands in the dirt, his knees in the earth. Something felt so natural about the act.

Nothing was spoken by anyone all that day. A natural collaboration seemed to flow between all involved, an understanding and companionship beyond the need for words. For the first time, Lam began to feel he had a place. He experienced a sense of belonging and having a purpose. His fear of the Others coming to take him began to melt away, taking his confusion with it.

He returned to the field at first light the next day, and was surprised to find the weeds had re-grown. This field apparently provided never ending work. As soon as one end was weeded, the first end needed picking again.

Silent nods and bows were exchanged between each new arrival, effectively acknowledging and respecting each other. Lam felt seen, and this caused a pleasant welling in his chest. He seemed to be accepted here, as if he had always come to tend this piece of land each day. He felt a lightness in his heart as he inhaled a deep breath and looked to the sky. He smiled as he studied the large cloud directly overhead. He found this productivity made him feel warm inside like when he was with his mother.

Just after mid-sun that day, he spotted his mother standing just inside the tree line, watching him. She made no move or gesture toward him, so he was unsure what he should do. He straightened and made it known he was aware of her presence. It occurred to him that he now thought of her as his mother, though he had no memories beyond three days ago, and had only been with her a very short time from his perspective.

Deciding to follow the cue from his fellow tenders, he nodded to her slightly, and bowed. Ric'ua stood motionless a few moments, then slowly declined her head in return before slipping back into the trees and out of sight.

That evening, Ric'ua embraced him tightly as he entered the door of their home. No words were spoken, but tears were allowed to flow freely down both their faces. The gesture spoke more than a million words as far as Lam was concerned.

After the weed plucking the following day, Lam decided to surprise Ric'ua and bring home as many gurja fruits as he could carry. He excitedly went bush to bush, following each new bunch of the bright yellow-green fruits he saw. Something felt very familiar about this. Perhaps he had done this same thing a thousand times before in the times he could not remember. He was aware of a prickling in the back of his mind. Pausing, he glanced around and found he had strayed farther from the field and village than he had realized. He looked up, and saw the faithful, huge cloud hanging overhead. If it held rain, surely it would begin dropping it at any moment now. Lam decided he better head back home.

He turned the direction he'd come from, and froze in his tracks.

There, still as the trees themselves, stood five people he immediately knew were not from his village. Although there were no outward indications, Lam knew who they were.

Others.

He felt them.

Tension immediately locked every muscle in Lam's body. He dropped his bundle of gurja fruits, and they went skittering across the ground. A thousand thoughts ran through his mind at once. Should he climb to the trees again? Bolt and make a run for it? Stand his ground and fight?

The others remained still as well, merely watching him with their firm, angry faces. Their lack of movement confused Lam. Did they not recognize him after all? Were his feelings they were Others wrong? Why did they simply stand there?

What felt like hours passed as the five and the one faced each other under the darkening canopy of tree leaves. It seemed each side was stubbornly determined to overpower the other by sheer force of will.

The spell was broken at last by a shout from behind the Others. One of the five turned and screeched a warbling call, which was returned again by the distant voice. The one that had responded to the call then abruptly came forward quicker than Lam expected, and grabbed his arm tightly. The other four parted and created a walk space for Lam to be dragged toward his village.

They were not going to hurt him? What had that signal meant? What had they been waiting for?

As they neared the village, a dull roaring sound and flickers of orange light on the trees soon showed Lam why the Others had acted as they had.

They had only been stalling him.

Their purpose had not been to hurt him, but to distract him, so other Others could set a home on fire. His home.

Everywhere, Lam's people were shouting and frantically rushing about trying to contain the flames lashing from his hut. Some inched as close as they dared, beating the flames with cloths and blankets. Some flung what little water they could find at it, clearly having no effect, but needing to assist by doing *something*. Some crouched between his house and the neighboring houses, as if to block the fire from spreading further with their very bodies.

A wailing and screaming rose above the roar and chaos, and Lam recognized it as Ric'ua's voice. He fought and kicked the Other who still gripped his arm. Twisting free, he charged for the hut his mother's voice was coming from. He had nearly reached the dwelling when he was slammed hard in the chest and flattened to the ground. A foot pressed into his throat, pinning him down.

"You will *not* enter our grounds again!" growled the menacing face that bent over Lam before spitting in his eye. "Next time, it will be the whole village," he leaned in even closer. "And *you* will be dead, you worthless son of Ric'ua." He released the pressure of his foot, and Lam gasped for air. "But what do you expect from the offspring of a mate-slave!"

The man ran off, disappearing into the shadows of the forest.

Lam coughed and wheezed as he fought his way back to his feet. Ric'ua's howling had never stopped, yet cut off mid-wail when Lam burst into the home.

"Pael!" she cried and threw her arms around him. "Pael! Oh Pael, I thought you were burned! Oh Pae—" She pulled back just enough to look into his eyes. A different sort of tears than they had cried only the night before streamed down their faces. "Lam…" she barely whispered. Her lips pressed into a tight, straight line as she shook her head.

"No," she spoke firmly, "You will always be my Pael."

SIX

After their hut had completely collapsed to nothing but ashes, Lam and Ric'ua were gifted the home they had taken shelter in, which Lam found belonged to a man named Terlikk. He recognized him immediately from the grove field. The man merely bowed to them, gathered his mate and two children, and left the mother and son alone.

Ric'ua had yet to let go of Lam, as if she were afraid he would be lost again if she released him. She pulled him to the floor with her and continued to hold him tight.

"I thought you to be lost once," she whispered to him finally. "When the messenger recognized you in the Gildok village and brought the word you had been caught, I feared the worst. Every bone in my body collapsed, and I fell as if dead.

"Why did you go as far as their village? Had you not heard the many warnings I and others pressed upon you? It was foolish to enter their land. Oh, but you have always been a fearless one. Even the truth that few have returned from their land alive did not frighten you.

"Yet I alone am to blame. If only I did not love the gurja fruit so much. If only I had not sent you out to gather for me. I knew in my heart you had risked yourself to bring me the best you could find. You are a good son. No mother could ever deny this.

"But when my ears heard you were being chopped down by the Gildoks…" Ric'ua's voice failed her, and Lam knew she was crying again. He felt helpless to comfort her.

Inhaling deeply to steady herself, she spoke again.

"When you did not return that night, I knew the messenger spoke the truth. My son was dead.

"I did not move from the earth all the next day. None could rouse me, no speech would console me. Word of your demise and my condition reached the Shen-Ma, and her spirits whispered to her. 'This is not the full truth,' she declared. 'Cast scouts to the east and find the boy, and bring the mother to me.'

"With great joy, they brought the news to me, but I refused to believe. Although I trusted our Shen-Ma, the dread was too much for me to bear. I did not rise.

"The men then lifted me. They carried me to the Shen-Ma. The Seer was intently preparing a large bonfire and muttering to herself. She did not even acknowledge my presence. I continued to lie in the dirt, though I watched her every move.

"As the sun grew low, a messenger ran into her courtyard as quickly as his feet could bear him. Gasping for breath, he announced they had found you on the land of the old Riglit tribe, sleeping in the dozime vines that have overtaken that dead village." Ric'ua laughed. "You were the dead, sleeping with the dead." She sighed before continuing. "The messenger said because they were unable to wake you, they were carrying you directly to the Shen-Ma themselves.

"The Shen-Ma clapped her hands in glee and said things were right on schedule as she slipped the boy a pouch of coins and sent him off to gather the rest of the village for a special ceremony.

"She then spoke to me for the first time. 'Ric'ua,' she said, 'You must prepare yourself. Change has come, and you must come to a new mind.' She then returned to her preparations.

"The people began arriving just as darkness settled. I found the strength to rise when the men arrived with your body. The Shen-Ma now had the fire in a blaze, and in its light I could see it really *was* you. My son was not lost!

"The people gathered around, and all could see, even as you slept, that you were different. Your essence was changed. Whispers of shock and anxiety rippled through the crowd. What had happened to Ric'ua's son?

"Our Seer began her ceremony. Calling the spirits from all directions, drawing up the soul of the earth, inviting in the heart of the skies, she requested all eyes be opened and all hearts be softened to the truths that lay before us, no matter what those truths may be revealed to be. The Shen-Ma grew still as a statue, and the air seemed to grow darker, the fire brighter. The wind increased until it howled through the trees. To me, the wind was mourning for my son. All these abruptly stopped when the Shen-Ma fell on you and placed her forehead to yours.

"Silence fell upon the crowd, in the same way she had fallen on you. None dared to breathe, and not even the smallest child moved a muscle. As one, we watched and waited, for though you had caused your share of trouble in the village, you were also loved and wanted and cared for. I sensed this from all those around me, and that alone kept me upright. I was not alone. I fear I would have returned to the earth otherwise," she sighed.

"You awoke and I nearly collapsed after all," she continued. "Even from the distance and in the shadowy firelight, I could see you were different. Something had changed." Her body shuddered against him in a silent sob. "You were no longer my son."

Ric'ua broke into full tears. Lam remained next to her, both allowing her to experience her emotion, and observing the emotion. He found it also caused a reaction in his own body. His own eyes welled up again as they had when he had been cornered in the tree.

Her weeping grew still, and they lay in silence.

"I don't remember anything before being in the tree," Lam whispered finally. "I thought I remembered *something*, at first… but even that has now gone.

"But I do feel a sense of familiar things. You feel the most… comfortable."

Ric'ua burst into tears again and pulled him to her even tighter. "Oh, Lam!" she exclaimed, "That was absolutely the most perfect thing you could have said to me!"

"You called me Lam…"

Her crying became laughter in a heartbeat. "Yes," she breathed, "I did, didn't I?"

SEVEN

Lam marveled at the unity he witnessed as all the people of the village abandoned their daily routines and worked to rebuild his and Ric'ua's home the next day. He was reminded how everyone had also done whatever they could to help put out the fire as it blazed the night before. A pressure in his chest grew into a lump in his throat. His eyes began crying again. He looked to Ric'ua standing beside him, and saw that she, too, was weeping openly.

He allowed his deep, dark eyes to drift of their own accord, taking in the luscious green trees with their arms to the skies and their roots in the ground. It felt as if they were standing guard around this tiny village nestled between the violent and the dead. He gazed at the radiant flowers of pinks, oranges, and blues, inhaling their fragrances even from where he stood. He admired the skill it had taken and the effort that had been put into the construction of the huts around him. He looked to the sky and smiled at the ever-present cloud. It had yet to release any rain, but nobody had seemed to notice. Lam had begun to think of it as a friend, always there with him, whether in a tree, falling asleep, working in the field, or connecting to the beauty he found himself in the midst of.

This place truly *was* beautiful.

Why had he ever been concerned about anything that came *before?*

Lam's sense of belonging continued to swell inside him, and he knew that he did love this place. He loved these people. They were a family. They were *his* family.

As the days and weeks went by, Lam eased more and more into the flow of the community. The more he took part, the more he realized just how interconnected this village was— with each other and with the land.

The weeks turned into months. He continued working the fields each morning. In the afternoons, Lam also began gathering fruit and nuts for the older people of the village who found it more and more difficult to walk far enough into the forest to gather their own. In the evenings, he adopted the responsibilities of collecting the waste remains from each hut, loading it all into a great, tightly-knit netting he could then drag to the compost area just beyond the western tree line of the village. The symbolism in this occurred to him more than once as he performed this task, and made him feel as if he were truly contributing to this society. He was taking care of the family. He was removing the harmful residue from the village. He was giving back what he felt they had given him— life.

On many occasions, Lam overheard others talking about him, unaware he was within earshot. They spoke of what a change in him they'd seen, even beyond his shift in essence. Where he had terrorized and destroyed the hard work of others, he now helped build and improve. Where he had mocked and humiliated, he now encouraged and uplifted. Had it been simple maturity, frightened into him by the Gildoks, or had something more magical happened to the boy? It was truly as if he were a different person.

Lam had nearly knocked the Shen-Ma over one day as he listened intently to one of these conversations. He looked into her eyes and saw that she, too, had heard the conversation, and saw she knew he had been listening as well. A flash of heat shot through his body. He knew he should not have been eavesdropping. And of all the people to catch him— the Seer herself!

Relief quickly replaced his embarrassment as the Shen-Ma simply smiled at him. "When the time is right," she said with a twinkle in her eye.

Had he really been that different before? He could not imagine even thinking such things he heard being remembered, much less doing them. Why *couldn't* he remember anything before that day in the tree? The answers to these remained as blank in his mind as the missing time itself.

One day, as he was helping an elderly neighbor cut freshly plucked gurja fruit, Lam froze mid-slice. His eyes had fallen upon a young woman crossing the central space before him. Her long, black hair fell well past her shoulders, and the skin of her arms wrapped around the basket she held seemed to be perfect and pure. His blade slipped from his hand as he watched her turn her body and maneuver around a group of children who had stumbled across her path. The flash of leg that emerged from her wrappings of maroon and gold as her feet darted to a clear path made his heart stop. She glanced his direction as the old woman he was helping began laughing and cackling uncontrollably. Lam and the girl's eyes met for a brief moment, and the image of her large, deep brown eyes was burned into his mind forever. Her full lips blessed him with a soft smile just before she turned and continued on her way. He knew instantly this was something he would *not* forget.

"Eh, heh heh! You like that, eh, boy?" the woman beside him poked his ribs before erupting into wild laughter again. "Ah, to be young again," she sighed.

"Who," Lam began, "Who is that?" The girl's hips swayed ever so slightly as she continued away from the central space, but not so slightly it escaped Lam's attention.

"That one is the daughter of Terlikk's brother."

Lam looked at the old woman quickly. The girl was related to their neighbor who had offered his home for them? Why had he never seen her before now? He opened his mouth to ask even as his elder offered the answer.

"The Shen-Ma sent for her from the distant Piktel village." She leaned close to him and whispered, "The word behind closed doors says she is in training to be the next Shen-Ma!"

"The next…" he trailed off, hypnotized once again by the grace of the young woman as she disappeared around the bend.

The old woman slapped the table they had set up, and laughed and laughed, fully enjoying the reaction she had just seen.

"But I wouldn't put it past our Shen-Ma to have even more plans for that girl." She winked at Lam, then returned to her fruit chopping.

"Do you know her name?" he asked.

"Ch'kara."

"Ch'kara," he whispered, smiling.

"Go on," the old woman crowed as she poked him again. "You know you want to follow her!" She waggled her fingers in the air. "I release you to flow with the wind!"

After studying her for a moment to see if she was truly serious or not, Lam wiped his hands of the gurja juice, and slowly went after the mysterious and beautiful girl.

His steps quickened as he rounded the last corner she had turned. He felt a broad smile spread across his face. He had never had this reaction to a girl before. He had seen the other girls around this village, and although they were very beautiful, none had caused him to feel these feelings. What was different about this one? Lam knew he would soon find out. His feet made a little hop of their own accord as he came into view of this leg of the village.

The young woman was nowhere to be seen. He stood in the middle of the pathway and looked all around, receiving several curious stares from the people tending to their chores. He looked back the way he came. Perhaps she had paused, and he had passed right by her in his musings.

He saw no sign of the girl.

Disappointed, he left the pathway, allowing both his mind and his feet to wander through the trees. Something inside him wanted to talk to the young woman *so* much, and not only talk to her— he felt to simply *be* in her presence would certainly be enough. He had seen adult couples in the village, men and women who were clearly quite attached to one another. More than once, Lam had wondered how they became that way. How did they select their mate? Were they arranged to be paired off without choice? Or was the choiceless nature of the matter the intense feelings of attraction such as he was feeling now? He felt this last must be the truth. The feelings felt *so* good— how could they be wrong?

Lam drifted back from his thoughts and realized he had stopped walking, and was staring up at the huge, pure white cloud. He felt a surge in his chest similar to what he had felt when he saw the girl. Now this was different. He'd seen the cloud overhead every day all these months, and had never felt this.

As he contemplated this, the cloud began growing larger. What was this? He had never seen it change its size or shape before either.

After a moment, Lam realized it wasn't growing at all, but descending! He was mesmerized as it sank lower and lower, until it came to a rest around the top of a particularly large tree so thickly that Lam could not see the treetop at all. Slowly, he stepped toward it, partly from curiosity, partly from the curious emotional pull of it.

His entire body felt as if it were buzzing with electricity. He approached the tree. He held his hand out, nearly touching the trunk, yet hesitant to go any further. Lam tilted his head to look into the branches. The urge to climb the tree and be *inside* the cloud was overwhelming.

The young woman, the village, his mother— all were forgotten as he grasped the lowest branch.

The moment he touched the tree, a jolt went through his system. *The top, come to the top,* echoed in his mind with such intensity he thought of nothing else, and began scrambling up as quickly as he could.

When his head entered the cloud, he was enveloped with a soothing and familiar sensation. *Come...* His climbing never slowed, until he was clinging to the barest and highest branch, just as he was in his first and earliest memories.

At first, he could see nothing but the thick whiteness all around. It occurred to him this situation would normally be frightening, yet he continued to feel warmly sedated and actually quite happy.

The clouds began to part and drift to each side. Startled, he looked down and saw his legs and feet remained solidly surrounded by cloud. He could clearly see the sky above him, but he could not see the ground below. He realized this meant no one below could see he was in the tree as well.

Lam looked to the sky again. A gasp escaped him as he realized he was no longer seeing the sky. In its place was a huge greyness. It seemed to be longer and wider than his entire village. Had the clouds returned that quickly, laden with a rainstorm ready to burst at any moment? Had he lost time again, and was now looking into the twilight sky? No, this was shiny and reflective— he could see the reflection of the treetops and himself in its hazy surface. It seemed like a metal, but did not look like the knives and farming tools the blacksmiths created from the metal of this land.

Lam did begin to feel scared now. What *was* this? Surely something so huge could destroy him and the entire area in one strike! What did it want?

Even as these thoughts ran panicking through his mind, the object began to change. It grew brighter, whiter. It condensed and seemed to shrink into itself, until it was nearly the size of Lam himself. Lam's mouth dropped open as he saw the object had taken

the shape of a body hovering mid-air before him.
   We did not mean to cause you fear.

• EIGHT •

He was not hearing the voice with his ears. The voice was in his head, but not the way his own thoughts were in his head. The voice simply *was*.

The human-shaped object floated in the air in front of Lam, bobbing slightly, and glowed with such a bright light he could not look at it directly. He took the risk of holding on to the tree branch with only one hand, and held the other hand up to shield his eyes. He squinted into the glare, but could make out no features beyond its shape.

"Who are you?" Lam called.

It is not necessary to use your voice. We hear your words.

"You hear…" he trailed off.

The energy which forms your thoughts is more than sufficient for us to hear. There is no need to speak aloud with us, yet this was to be expected. If it is easier for you in your current condition, you may speak with physical sounds.

Lam was speechless for a long while. The light patiently waited.

"Who are you?" he finally asked again.

We are you. You are of us. And from us.

"F-from you?"

Yes. Though it is clear you have not been able to remember, still it remains with you. Search within yourself. See what you find. Breathe in the air. We will help.

Lam took a deep breath. He still felt calm and at ease. No fear, anxiety, or tension was in his body, yet he found no insight. He shook his head.

Silently, the light reached out the shape of an arm, and touched Lam in the center of his chest. All suddenly went dark. There was a large fire burning high nearby. He tried to turn to see what was on fire, but found he could not move. A cackling laughter brought his attention back to center just as the face of an old woman leaned close to his. The Shen-Ma. He was still underneath the Seer, that first night? Had he lost consciousness and dreamed these past months? How could that be? Lam *knew* he had experienced all these days. Moments with Ric'ua, weeding the field, helping the neighbors— they had all been *real*, he was sure of it!

"SEED!"

The blinding light was before him once again, filling all his senses. He was back at the top of the tree, struggling to catch his breath. Looking down, he saw cloud rather than crowd, and breathed a sigh of relief. This was the present moment, and not his first moment of being chopped down.

Have you found it?

He turned to the light. He knew what it wanted him to say, but did he believe it? Could it possibly be true? He had dismissed and nearly forgotten the Shen-Ma's words as he became a part of the village community.

They seemed too impossible to even entertain. Yet a floating metallic light from a cloud was very convincing evidence that it *could* very well be true.

"I am the seed of the stars," he whispered.

You are.

Lam and the light silently stared at each other, if the light had eyes. It seemed perfectly willing to simply wait for him to draw his conclusions and choose his reactions. Even with the confirmation of the Shen-Ma's words he had just received, he still felt completely at peace. In this moment, it did feel as if it could be true, whether the presence of the light was the only reason for these feelings, or if there was another factor at work he was unaware of. What would Ric'ua think? How would she react? They had never once brought up the subject of that night. Lam had been so overjoyed that his mother had accepted and embraced him, he had always been careful to never do or say anything that could jeopardize that.

Something suddenly occurred to him, and he finally broke the silence.

"This cloud," he began. "It's always been… you, hasn't it?"

We have never been apart from you. From the moment you crossed the barrier, we have always been with you.

"Why do you hide in the cloud?"

The cloud is illusion. It was decided by The Remnant to disguise our presence as such, until the conditions were acceptable.

"Am I the only…"

No. The light responded before his question was fully out. *All can see the cloud, but only you can see to its core. You are the one who chose this.*

"I *chose* this?" Lam asked, bewildered.

You are of The Remnant. You were who wished to activate this transition. Not all were in agreement, yet it was decided.

"I was… what? I decided? I sent… myself?"

You are The First.

Lam shook his head. "No," he said. "That's not true. This is ridiculous— I must be dreaming." He began climbing down. The light made no move or word to stop him.

He hopped to the ground and began walking quickly back toward the village, glancing up only once to see that the cloud was still low around the tree. He could see only cloud from down here. "Ridiculous," he muttered again.

Lam burst from the tree line and was bounced off his feet to the ground. Astonished, he looked up to see a large, round figure. He had run straight into the Shen-Ma!

He was immediately embarrassed, and began scrambling to his feet, then froze. The radiant girl was standing beside the Seer. Both women were simply smiling at him.

"I-I'm so sorry!" he stammered.

"Where have *you* been, son of Ric'ua?" the Shen-Ma asked.

"I," he swallowed. The presence of the young woman was having a strange effect on his body. "I was just taking a walk."

The Shen-Ma turned to the girl and grunted a noise that sounded more like an animal than an old woman. The two then burst into giggles together. Lam merely stood still, awkwardly unsure what to do. He watched the women in wonder.

They turned and began walking away from him at a pace that he knew to be typical for the Shen-Ma. The old one paused and beckoned for him to follow.

"She has something to tell you," said the girl before she turned as well.

Hearing the sound of her voice for the first time was more than enough to set Lam's feet instantly in motion.

• NINE •

Lam sat down on the log next to the girl. He was not sure what to do or say, but the Shen-Ma had firmly indicated they were to sit, then disappeared into her hut. She had not returned. But Lam was thoroughly enjoying the closeness of the girl, and did not mind at all.

"I am Ch'kara," the girl finally broke the silence with her beautiful voice.

"I know," he said before thinking.

"Oh?"

The heat of embarrassment instantly rushed to his ears. "I, uh…" The smile on her face stopped him, and he realized she was playing with him.

"I knew you knew of me," she giggled. "I was brought here for you."

Ch'kara bust into giggles at the sight of his gaping mouth. He quickly shut his mouth and broke into a grin himself.

"Old Pa'cha said you are to be our next Shen-Ma."

She looked shyly away. "That is part truth."

"Part?" he asked, then remembered her earlier hint. "For… me."

She snuck a look at him, then grabbed a stick and began poking the fire before them with it. Lam wasn't sure why the Shen-Ma kept her fire going constantly, even when it was warm and sunny out. It was simply one of the quirks one did not show the disrespect of asking about. Perhaps it was a secret. The Seer *did* seem to have certain spells and magic others did not.

"You are free to ask anything, son of Ric'ua." The old woman had emerged silently from her hut and come beside them. She began combining items into a small wooden bowl. Lam startled, but found his wandering mind had lost its thoughts. He had no questions, yet now felt compelled to ask something, so as not to offend his elder.

"Why do you never say my name?"

The Shen-Ma paused her preparations and turned to him, unsmiling. She looked directly in his eyes as if she were reading something there. Lam broke the gaze to glance at Ch'kara. She was still smiling broadly.

He turned back to the old woman as she whispered, "I will answer both your questions. The fire burns so that we may live. This village, these people depend on it." She fed the flames a twig with three leaves on it, as if to demonstrate for him, or perhaps in offering to it for revealing its purpose. "At this moment you are neither Pael nor Lam." She returned her focus to the bowl. Lam was speechless. Ch'kara silently reached over and took his hand in hers, sending tingles throughout his body. The Shen-Ma chuckled as if she saw what had just happened, though her back was turned to them.

"You were talking to *Them*, weren't you, boy?"

"Them?"

"You know," the Shen-Ma prodded, "The Clouds."

"The Stars," he murmured.

"Exactly." She held the bowl directly over the fire for a moment, whispering something under her breath before dumping its contents into the blaze and leaping back, all at once. Without looking, she plopped to the end of the log beside Lam. He barely had time to scoot over and make room for her before she landed. He scooted directly against Ch'kara.

Pretending to be oblivious to what she had just caused, the Shen-Ma heaved a long sigh and gazed at the stars.

"The stars," she mused. "Long have we looked to the stars for our hope. It seems it should be an odd thing to place one's hope in things so very far away, something so remote, something so *separate* from us. Ah, but that is the key, isn't it? There *appears* to be a separation between us and the stars, but we do not *feel* as if there is any separation. We feel close to them. We feel we *know* them.

"The Ancients acknowledged this, you know. They taught that in the beginning, when only animals walked this ground, *They* arrived. The ones from the stars. There are many, many stories of those who came. Some tell they were actual gods with magical and mystical powers, creating the people from invisible nothingness. And there are still other stories that say the people grew on their own, over vast amounts of time— grew from the tiniest specks of life energies left behind by those from the stars. But throughout all the various interpretations, the one detail that remains constant is *we came from the stars.*

"There are many who cling to the thought *'This is not our home'* with desperate abandon. For whatever hardships and difficulties they find here, they choose to believe there is something *better* apart from this place. Many of these people are simply attempting to avoid responsibility for their own lives, and in doing so, waste away what life they *do* have here, all the while pining for something *else* that may or may not exist.

"Yet there are those of us," she continued, "Who believe these things for a very different reason. There are those of us who *know* the truth in these stories that have been passed from generation to generation. We feel it in our bones.

"Our line, our ancestors— in whatever form— began in the stars." The Shen-Ma shifted sideways, granting Lam and Ch'kara an opportunity to move apart, which they did not take.

"Each and every one of us is not directly from the stars, you understand, but we are each from the stars in the way of our beginnings." She grew silent, and dropped her eyes from the sky to the fire. Lam and Ch'kara waited patiently, perfectly content being close to each other, as if they had always been this way.

"Do you understand who you are, son of Ric'ua?"

Lam knew the answer she was searching for, though he did not feel it completely in his body. "The cloud said the same as you, Shen-Ma," he said. "I am the Seed."

"The Seed," she repeated, nodding.

"He needs to be told," Ch'kara spoke next to him. He was very aware she was still holding his hand as he turned back to the old woman for her response.

The Shen-Ma sighed and lifted her eyes to the stars once again. "Long ago, a wise Ancient named L'karta performed a very special ceremony. This ceremony had never been carried through before. He must have received it directly from the stars, for it released his spirit from his body, and he rose high above this land. No other had ever done this before. From this perspective, he saw the land was actually curved and not flat at all. He saw there were other rocks—countless rocks— all seemingly suspended in between the endless stars. He looked down and saw the souls of the people below, shining as many different colors, a living tapestry, each connected to the next. There were no gaps in this Quilt of Life.

"He was met by three spirits who claimed to be of the stars. They encircled L'karta's soul, and lifted him higher and higher, taking him to their own curved land under a sun that was not our own. Here, they imparted to him all manner of knowledge and wisdom in a matter of mere hours. It was as if they simply opened his mind and poured their words inside! He remembered no speech or audible sounds at all.

"He was returned, and was placed beside his bonfire, as if he'd never left. Naturally, many believed he had only dreamed the experience and it had not truly happened." The Shen-Ma chuckled. "It is said he responded, 'Of course I dreamed it— how else has any of my work been accomplished?'" She cackled fully out loud now, and Lam knew her own experience made the Ancient's reply so hilarious to her. He cracked a smile himself, and imagined Ch'kara was doing the same, though he did not want to risk a glance to find out.

"From that journey, he brought back a message. He foretold that one directly from the stars would come into our midst. This one would once again unite all the people into the Quilt of Life he beheld from above, arriving when the need was greatest, when the violence was its most pointless and most heartless. It was said this one would come out of this heartless land, and plant the seed that would change the nations. A Seed would be planted, and this seed would never be crushed for ages to come." She smiled a secretive smile to herself as she adjusted the logs of her bonfire with the tip of her walking stick.

"L'karta was my direct ancestor. He was a grandfather who is with me, even this day, though he has refused to impart to me any further insight from the other worlds," she sighed.

"The spirits love games, you know," she said, "Especially games with words. I thought I understood exactly what the prophecy said, what it meant. Of all the wisdom passed to me, I closed my mind to the most important." The old woman laughed again. "I decided I had learned all I could on that prophecy, and had bound any new power from entering it!

"But now I see." She turned and smiled directly at Lam, before meeting Ch'kara's eyes. It was apparent the two women had already had conversation on what the old one was about to say.

"I had thought the one from the stars would be born to the violent tribes, such as the Gildoks, or the Furds further north. I believed they would change the violent ones from within, then emerge to unite us all. I see now I was only partly right in this. You came from our own people, went *to* the Gildoks, and emerged, changed yourself.

"In a way, you *were* born in the Gildok land. As Pael, Ric'ua's only son, and her only family, after your father's encounter with the same Gildoks so many seasons ago, you ventured too far into the forest yourself. You slipped from their grasp only long enough to climb a tree. Yet this did not stop them, for that fierce tribe is not known to stop for anything once their minds are set to a thing. They began to tear you down from below, plucking the roots right from you.

"They tore your soul right from your body.

"So overtaken by the energy of the Gildok people's fear and anger, Pael chose to release this body of his own accord, rather than let the cruel ones take it. This opened the path for Lam to enter, taking the body as its own, for purposes of its own— the purpose of Planting!

"Lam was born from the violence and harmful desires of others."

Lam was speechless. The Shen-Ma sat silently.

"How," he finally began, "How is this possible?"

"How is it possible for the clouds to talk?" the old one replied.

He thought on this, feeling at once a sinking feeling and a thrill of excitement. "From the stars…" he whispered. "I am from the stars."

"Do you remember?"

He closed his eyes, searching within himself. He found no specific memories, but suddenly touched the sense of something *before* once again. Slowly, he began to nod his head. "I feel it is true…"

"Then perhaps you should look above you."

Lam opened his eyes and looked up to find the cloud had come over them, and had descended so close he could reach up and touch it. He gasped and looked quickly to Ch'kara. Her head had slumped to her chest, yet rose and fell slightly with her breathing, fast asleep. He turned to the Shen-Ma and saw she merely sat firmly and silently, watching his reactions, revealing no hint of her own reactions.

The wind began to swirl around them, stirring the dust and leaves. The fire writhed as if in agony. A soft rumble rapidly grew into a loud roar as a continuous thunder broke all around them. Lam felt the vibration of it to his very bones. He felt no fear, yet sat unmoving, looking into the cloud.

Sparks of light began to flash randomly throughout the cloud as the wind whipped more and more fiercely. The sparks grew bigger and lit longer, until they were full streaks of lightning shooting from one end of the cloud to the other, side to side, top to bottom. The cloud rolled and boiled, turned inward on itself, and rushed back out.

Suddenly a single bolt of lightning shot from the direct center of the cloud and struck Lam in the direct center of his forehead.

TEN

He was not alone.

He could not see the others around him. He had no eyes with which to see them, but he knew they were there. He didn't know from a memory— he *felt* them.

They were in a circle, yet they were not standing. They had no bodies with which to stand. Each of the others were merely spaces of presence around him. He quickly realized he, too, was simply an energetic presence, and a part of the circle.

This place was a room, but not a room. He could sense no walls or boundaries to it, as if it continued infinitely in every direction. At the same time, it felt like a confined space, a certain *place.* He felt another aspect present here as well, a sort of tingling electric charge filling the space, as if anything that was said or done in this place would instantly spark into life.

He had drifted off. Had he been sleeping? He thought he had. He'd been dreaming, too. It had been a very nice dream, something about a forest and a village. A warm feeling swept through him at the memory. He felt like smiling, but he had no face here. That had only been in the dream, hadn't it?

Do you remember now? one of the others asked silently. *Have you found it?*

I fell asleep.

We do not sleep here.

But I did. I even had a dream. I had a body, and a mother, and—

He does not remember.

He must be conscious of both sides in order to intentionally activate the cycle!

He should not have gone.

It was his choice. No other took his free will.

Go? I was… not here?

Your presence was removed, Lam.

You were no longer among us.

I… Images of tree and cloud and fire flashed through his awareness. *Do you mean…* Faces shifted into his mind, then quickly faded into other faces—angry faces, smiling faces, worried faces, old faces. *That truly happened?*

You chose to descend.

You lowered the vibration of your being.

You merged with the body, just as those long before.

You made the transition.

Clarity shot through Lam as full connection returned. Memories that were embedded within the substance of his energy sprang to life as he in mere nanoseconds relived the long history of a crumbling society and its eventual destruction. The wars, the struggles, the pure energetic pain so many others caused tore through his awareness. The efforts of the few had made no difference as those who bewilderingly chose isolation outweighed the balance, and ultimately set the final dissolution into motion.

Waiting until the last possible moment, the few who sought to cherish their kind had finally separated their existence from the collective, and set out to begin a new society. Their awareness was twelve in number, and if they had not been willing to leave before the dissolution had completed, bearing the memories and knowledge of their society, there would no longer be any trace of their kind. They were now The Remnant.

As ages passed, they began to sense a new imbalance.

Although they held the information of their kind in its entirety, they alone were not complete. They found their energy had been siphoned away, iota by iota. The limited cycles of an incomplete collective were not enough for the energy to recycle and rebuild itself. They needed a base point for an inclusive beginning, and they were running out of time to find it.

It was agreed joining a lower vibrational species would be the best chance of their survival— a return to the very root of existence was better than a total loss of their awareness.

The first beings they had encountered had already advanced farther than Lam and The Remnant would have liked, but, in their desperation, had chosen to proceed.

Four of them had been selected to descend and transition into their midst. The plan was to cohabit the existing structures and bodies of the beings, and begin to spread among them, providing a complete cycle for their energy essence to flow freely through. At first, it seemed they had found salvation, but time revealed another outcome— the vibrational structure of the beings proved to be too high to accept a permanent merging. The four pioneers were repeatedly disconnected from their hosts, kicked out over and over until they were finally rejected completely.

They were too dissipated by that point to be able to return to The Remnant.

After such a loss, Lam and the other cherishers were much more cautious in their planning, and all the more hesitant to attempt further vibrational transitions.

They had found three other potential societies before coming to this solar system. Long periods of observation had offered no clues of a solution for them, and brought The Remnant to the decision of passing on all three.

Their time had now nearly expired.

When this place had been discovered, the long, routine observation period began again. Although this was by far the lowest vibrational, least evolved society they had encountered, the remaining eight of The Remnant knew that, success or failure, this was their last stop.

Lam specifically had reached the point of willingness to risk his own awareness for the sake of the group, and when he recognized that the beings of this place were repeating the same pattern he had seen send his own society spiraling into dissolution, it had sealed his decision to descend. He would attempt a cohabitation.

When the body of the one called Pael was seen to be abandoned, the action of entering the body was no sooner thought than done, and the detail of no other awareness inhabiting the body simultaneously proved to be just the key to a successful transition.

Lam refocused his full awareness to the seven around him.

I have found it. We are saved.

• ELEVEN •

"You found it? Good! Now get up— quick!"

Lam slowly opened his eyes to find he was back beside the fire, lying on his back. Twilight had settled around them. He had fallen backwards off the log, but his legs remained draped over it. Ch'kara was awake and kneeling over him with a concerned look on her face. Her expression quickly shifted to relief as she saw he had regained consciousness.

The Shen-Ma stood over his other side. Her walking stick was poised to jab him if necessary. The expression she wore was one of deep sadness that did not shift as she lowered her stick to the ground.

"Lam," she said.

"You mean 'Son of Ric'ua,'" he laughed, feeling much more confident than before.

The Shen-Ma's frown only deepened.

"No. You are now Lam, for the reason of you have now fully embraced and accepted your destiny," she paused and sighed, "And for the reason of you are no longer the son of Ric'ua."

Lam sat upright. "Because I am not Pael."

"Because Ric'ua no longer lives."

He leapt to his feet. "What are you saying?"

The old woman turned slightly away and did not answer for a moment. He looked to Ch'kara and saw it was apparent she was just as surprised as he was by this information. He looked to the sky and saw the cloud was now nowhere to be seen.

His eyes returned to the Shen-Ma as she heaved a tremendous sigh.

"The Gildok tribe has once again attacked our peaceful village while we have been here. Though all were innocent, most have not survived," she wiped tears from her cheeks, "Including your mother."

"What? How is this possible? How do you know?" he demanded. "Why did you not tell me, and let me go *help…*?" He trailed off as Ch'kara placed her hand on his shoulder.

"This was needed, now more than ever," the old woman whispered. "Sometimes the Great Way also involves great loss." She sat heavily to the log, visibly exhausted. He had never seen the Seer this way. "I brought you here because it was time. There was no more time.

"And now it is time once again. You are ready." She looked up and met his eyes.

"Was…" he slowly said, afraid of the answer, "Was this done… because of… me?" Images of the previous flames consuming his home flashed through his mind.

She shook her head. "No, Lam. This one was not because of you." She waved her hand in the direction of the village. "Go. Be the Seed."

Ch'kara sat beside the old woman to indicate she intended to stay. Lam looked toward the village, then back at the women. Both turned their backs to him.

He felt a panic in his chest as he broke into a run. How could this be real? Things had just begun to feel as if they were falling into place. A loving mother, a place in the community, a promising romantic relationship with a beautiful girl, and the discovery of answers to his own life— how could this have happened now?

Tears swam in the corners of his eyes as Lam raced through the forest as fast as he could, dodging tree branches and bushes. He stepped in a hole and fell to his knees. The cry that escaped his lips as he went down startled him. He intentionally yelled again in frustration as he scrambled back up and continued on.

He broke through the tree line and stopped in his tracks.

There were no fires, no smoke. There were not even any broken or crushed huts that he could see. But there was silence. Unnatural stillness.

And there were bodies.

The people who should have been quite active, even at this evening hour, preparing the village for the night, now lay in various places, at awkward angles. He saw no blood on the ground or on the clothes. There was no evidence of cuts or bruises on the bodies, yet still they lay there, clearly dead.

"No, no, no!"

He bolted for his own hut, side-stepping and jumping over the fallen. He yanked down the animal skin door covering and burst inside.

His mother lay unmoving on the ground, her arm outstretched toward the doorway.

Lam dropped to his knees. He remained speechless and unmoving, unable to take his eyes from Ric'ua.

Suddenly, he threw back his head and screamed.

Lam screamed the scream of one who has lost and lost and lost. He ran out of breath, clenched his fists tighter, inhaled another lungful of air, and screamed again. Again and again he yelled and cried and howled, pouring every ounce of anguish and anger into the sounds.

When he could cry no more, and had no voice left to scream with, Lam slowly stood. He gathered up the animal skin, and laid it over Ric'ua's body.

"Goodbye, mother," he whispered.

He emerged to find Ch'kara sitting on the ground in front of the hut, her legs crossed and her head low.

"Lam," she began.

He lifted a hand, stopping her.

"The Shen-Ma is gone as well, isn't she?"

Ch'kara nodded, and collapsed into the dirt.

• TWELVE •

Lam rushed to Ch'kara in desperation. He had already lost seemingly everything else in this life, he would *not* lose her as well.

The urge to flee this place was nearly overwhelming, and he could not shake the feeling of being watched, yet still he took the time to attempt to wake this young woman he felt such a pull to. If the Gildoks were still here, they would have to take him in order to get to her. These feelings overrode the fear pumping through his body.

Had she become victim to the same thing that had killed the rest of the people? No, he could see she was still breathing, which allowed him to release his breath again.

Unable to rouse Ch'kara, yet unable to sit in the open any longer, Lam gathered her limp body and lifted her in his arms. He turned in a circle, and decided that heading east, away from the Gildok land, was the best choice.

He set off into the trees, scrambling along the rocks, leaves, and fallen tree branches as quickly as he could. The electricity of his adrenaline and fear flowed freely, empowering his racing legs and mind. Why was there no blood to be seen on any of the bodies? How had the Gildoks done this monstrous deed? The Shen-Ma had known what was happening, yet had done nothing. Why was *that?*

Lam looked up through a small clearing as he passed by, and saw the cloud was not above him. Had it been overhead in the village? He'd been too distracted to notice, but did remember it had been gone when he woke beside the Shen-Ma's fire.

Had The Remnant left him as well?

Lam shoved these thoughts from his mind. He could not handle if even they had gone. If Ch'kara did not survive this, he would truly be alone. Looking down at her face again, he was overcome with both a feeling of love for her and the fear of losing her. Tears streamed down his face as the emotions formed a whirlwind within him.

Suddenly, Lam stopped in his tracks. He struggled to control and silence his labored breathing as he tilted his head and listened intently to the sounds around him.

Had that been voices he'd just heard?

Now that he stood still, Ch'kara's weight pulled at his arms. He strained to maintain a tight hold on her yet remain aware of the forest around him.

A low tone reached his ears, briefly rising, then falling, definitely the sound of voices speaking— and growing louder.

Lam searched his surroundings in alarm. He dashed behind a fallen tree and carefully laid Ch'kara on the ground behind it before laying beside her himself. He grabbed a branch of thick fern leaves and pulled it across the top of them just as the source of the voices came into view.

Peeking over the tree log, Lam saw three heads moving slowly along. They spoke softly to each other. Their manner seemed to be calm, yet cautious, as if aware things could change at any moment.

Lam raised himself a bit more to try to see the people's clothing. If these were Gildok, he knew he may end up having to fight, and he wasn't sure he had the strength left for that.

The people abruptly stopped and turned his direction. Lam quickly dropped fully behind the log, cursing under his breath. Had they heard him? He shut his eyes tight and held his breath, listening.

After moments of nothing but the natural sounds of the forest, he began to wonder if they had moved on, but he had not heard any footsteps. He willed his body to relax its tension, and wait a bit longer.

Strong hands suddenly grabbed him and yanked him to his feet. Beside him, Ch'kara's body was lifted as well. Lam released a shout as loud as his hoarse voice would allow, and began swinging his fists and kicking his feet. A second pair of hands quickly caught his legs and held him fast. He bucked and twisted and screamed all the more.

"Whoa, whoa!" one of the men said. "Easy! We will not hurt you, son of Ric'ua!"

Lam grew still and took his first close look at the men. He recognized the one holding his legs from the grove field. The one holding Ch'kara's unconscious body also looked vaguely familiar. He could not clearly see the man holding his own upper body, but he saw the clothing they wore were from his own village.

"You are the son of Ric'ua?" asked the one

holding Ch'kara.

"I know he is," replied the one holding Lam's arms, before he could respond for himself, "And that one you hold is the daughter of my brother!"

It was Terlikk, the neighbor who had offered them his home when fire had been set to their own! "I thought all had perished..." Lam whispered, sinking into the man's arms.

"We are very much alive," Terlikk laughed sadly, "And were afraid *you* were the ones who were dead!"

"But... how did you escape the Gildoks?"

The man who held his feet answered as he set them down. "We were nearest the edge of our village clearing when they attacked, yet still we barely escaped with our lives."

"What has happened to my niece?" Terlikk asked.

Lam was grateful to see the one who held Ch'kara was now supporting her head. "We were with the Shen-Ma when we heard the village was being attacked again. Ch'kara stayed with the Shen-Ma while I ran to help defend the people." He sank to the ground again, and leaned against the fallen tree.

"I was too late."

Terlikk sat on the log beside him, and placed a gentle hand on Lam's shoulder as he continued. "There were bodies everywhere, I thought the whole village had been murdered. I ran for my own home, and," a sob escaped him, "Found my mother was among the... gone."

"I am sorry for your loss," Terlikk said softly.

Lam nodded his thanks and inhaled deeply before continuing. "Ch'kara was waiting for me when I came out from covering my mother. She bore news of the Shen-Ma's fate, which she revealed to me before collapsing herself."

Terlikk heaved a sigh a relief. "That is at least one fortunate thing from this cursed day. My fear was Ch'kara had been infected by the Gildok potion as well. She will be all right after a rest then, I believe." He motioned to the man holding her. "Lay her back down, Feltin. You and Julak put together a cradle. We can carry her with us easier that way."

Turning back to Lam, he asked, "You are saying the Shen-Ma is gone as well?"

Lam nodded.

Terlikk's head dropped. "Was it the Gildoks?"

"No, I don't think so, but I don't know any more than Ch'kara told me. You know how the Gildoks killed our people without shedding their blood? You said they had a potion?"

"Yes," Terlikk nodded. "It had been said they had an alchemist among them, but it was not taken seriously." He sighed once again. "Yet I saw with my own eyes more of that cursed tribe than I have ever seen in one place before, rushing into our village and splashing a potion in the faces of every man, woman, and child they could find." He visibly shuddered and wiped tears from his face. "Each one the potion touched instantly and silently dropped to the ground, and moved no more.

"Now I believe they had an alchemist."

"Were…" Lam hesitated. "Were your mate and children…"

Terlikk looked away.

"I'm sorry," Lam said softly.

Julak and Feltin returned, dragging a sled of large leaves they had quickly woven together.

"We should keep moving, Terlikk. We need to get

back to the others before nightfall."

Lam looked up. "Others? You're not the only ones who escaped?"

"No, there are ten of us," Feltin replied.

"And now there are twelve," Terlikk corrected.

Lam nearly smiled.

"A remnant."

• THIRTEEN •

The more Lam thought about all that had happened, the angrier he became.

By the time they had reached the camp, his entire body had gone stiff and rigid. He felt heat all through his veins, and had an intense urge to take action. He kept his full feelings and thoughts to himself, and the others assumed he was merely saddened by the loss of his mother. They allowed him the space to process the emotions.

Those who had escaped the village had set up camp just outside a cave hidden behind a curtain of dozime vines. So the fires could also be hidden inside the shelter and not attract unwanted attention, someone had climbed nearly to the top of the hanging vines, and chopped a hole in them to allow the smoke from the fires an outlet.

Lam had been welcomed warmly, and there had been rejoicing that more of their people had been found. Stories and perspectives were swapped around the fire as the group got to know each other better with these new circumstances they found themselves in. Ch'kara had been laid nearby, and Lam checked on her constantly, but still she slept on. Discussions about what was expected to happen and what should be done next were held, and the opinions and ideas of everyone present were listened to with respect. Lam found he was very grateful for the sense of unity with these people. The shared experience had formed an instant bond among them. It was as if they were a little family. He remembered that was what it had been like within The Remnant as well, after the loss of their society.

Finally, the talking came to an end, and each of the twelve began to find a comfortable place to stretch out for the night. It was decided that one of them should remain awake through the night and keep watch. They did not know if the Gildoks knew some had escaped their cruelty or not, but if the violent tribe *did* know they had escaped, it had to also be expected they were out hunting for them. Feltin volunteered to keep watch this first night, though he had been on foot searching the nearby forest with Terlikk and Julak most of the day.

Even when all was quiet and still, Lam found he could not sleep. Laying protectively beside Ch'kara, his mind raced, and his emotions insisted that something be done. His new memories told him he had seen this happen again and again. It seemed as if everything everywhere merely repeated itself. Mirrors of mirrors, patterns of patterns— even in societies ages and worlds apart.

There *had* to be a way to stop the cycles.

He thought of The Remnant. He thought his origins. He thought of who he was, who he had become, and what had happened now. He now knew he was not like the others. He truly had not come from this place. But he was in this place now, and what happened here affected him just as much as the others.

The Shen-Ma had seen him to be a Seed, and his people in the cloud had confirmed it. What did that mean? What could he *do?*

The continuation of his original society depended on him, and now perhaps this mirrored remnant he was now a member of depended on him as well. They were the representation and all that was left of their village, weren't they?

But what was he to *do?*

By daylight, Lam had reached the decision he could not *not* do something. He was not from here, and therefore should have the benefit of that working to his advantage.

He would avenge the village.

He would make the Gildok tribe pay for what they did to his mother.

Ch'kara woke after they had all eaten their fill of gurja fruit and other berries they had found nearby, and were deciding the goals for the day. Lam was at her side in an instant. He found himself genuinely smiling for the first time as he looked down on her.

"Where… Where are we?" she asked.

"We've taken shelter in a cave," Lam replied. "Ten others survived the raid, and have taken us in. Your uncle is here."

"Thank you for not leaving me," she whispered.

"Thank *you* for not leaving *me*," he whispered in return.

"Ch'kara!" Terlikk knelt opposite Lam. "How are you feeling, dear niece?"

She nodded as she took Lam's hand to raise and sit. "Much better, Uncle."

Terlikk placed his hand on her shoulder. "I am relieved to find you are not only alive but well— I have survived yet another Gildok attack, but I may not have survived the wrath of my brother if I had lost his only child!"

Ch'kara broke into a smile as she twisted to embrace him. "I am the Shen-Ma," she said. "It will take more than that to be rid of me now."

"The Shen…" Terlikk and Lam spoke at once, in wonder.

The young woman nodded mischievously.

"Then," Terlikk said, "The Shen-Ma was not killed?"

She shook her head.

"She passed."

"But *how* did she pass on?" Lam asked.

Ch'kara fully giggled now as Terlikk solved her game. "The Shen-Ma *did* pass on," he said, "But furthermore, she *passed*— to Ch'kara!"

She lowered her eyes and sighed. "I grew very close to her in the short time I had with her, and am heartbroken she is no longer with us," she looked up and met Lam's eyes. "But one thing I do know is there are greater things to be done. When Lam embraced who he was, and what he came to do, I felt all else click into place as well. I knew then that I, too, was ready for what I am here to do."

"And what is that?" asked Lam. She merely smiled and stared into the distance.

"Well, I imagine we'll all find out soon enough," her uncle said. "Why don't you go see if the others need any assistance, Lam, and let us discuss some of our family matters. We've lost so much…"

Lam bowed as they had in the grove field, and left

them to their talk. His eyes went immediately to the skies as he exited the cave. The cloud was still not overhead. Where had they gone? Why had The Remnant abandoned him, especially now that he remembered and accepted he had come from them?

He wandered deeper in the forest. When he thought he had gone far enough from the others, he climbed to the top of a tree and shouted into the sky, "WHERE ARE YOU? WHY HAVE YOU LEFT ME? WHY DO I NO LONGER HAVE YOUR SUPPORT??"

Tears welled in his eyes as a mixture of sadness and anger boiled in his stomach. He felt utterly alone. He had Ch'kara, who seemed as if she intended to stay with him, but still, he was different. He could not shake the sinking feeling that he would always be alone in that way.

"SHOW YOURSELVES!!" he screamed as the anger once again reached a peak.

No response was given.

Lam climbed back to the ground, and headed back toward the cave in both disgust and a new resolve.

He was a member of The Remnant, a Cherisher from another star system. It was not only his duty to carry on the memory and knowledge of his people, it was expected of him. If the others of The Remnant had now left, then the entire fate of his society rested completely on him. He would transfer all the knowledge he had to the village remnant, and merge the customs of the two. His people would live on among these people.

Ch'kara met him a short distance from the camp. She stood looking tall and strong, completely refreshed. In her right hand she held a walking stick the height of her head.

They stood facing each other silently for a few moments, communicating with their eyes in almost the same way he had communicated with the others in the cloud. A calmness and understanding seemed to pass between them, and Lam felt a bond unmistakably present.

Finally, he motioned toward her walking stick. "You are the new Shen-Ma then," he said. "That is very much like the one the old Shen-Ma had."

"I am *the* Shen-Ma, Lam, and yet I am also still Ch'kara." She reached out and laid her palm to his cheek. "Her essence passed to me. I bear her memories as well."

Images of the cherishing he and the others had done within his own society flashed through Lam's mind. The collecting of knowledge for the purpose of carrying on that knowledge seemed similar to what Ch'kara was saying had been done here.

He simply smiled in understanding as she took his arm, and together they walked toward the cave.

"You know it will be dangerous," Ch'kara said just before they reached the cave. Lam stopped and looked at her. "To go back, for any reason."

He chuckled that she had read his mind just as the Shen-Ma used to, but nodded. "I know."

"I'm sorry about your mother."

Lam held her hand as they joined the others.

FOURTEEN

"That is *not* a good idea."

Terlikk crossed his arms in front of his chest to emphasize his seriousness as several others voiced their agreement. As they sat around the fire once again after a day of scouting and gathering, Lam had expressed his feelings and his plans to go after the Gildoks.

"That is foolishness," Terlikk stated, "And asking for danger."

Lam had been prepared for the others to not agree with him. It had been the same with the others of The Remnant. But, as with that greater mirror, he simply could not bring himself to take what felt like unnecessary risks for the larger whole, even if it meant risk to himself. He felt responsible for others— his people, and these people, who were now his people. He was not about to let another society be destroyed as his own had been. He knew that if the Gildoks were left untouched, that is exactly what would happen.

Terlikk saw Lam was unmoved by both his words and his body language, and relaxed his posture. "Lam," he said. "To go into such a situation without a base support— without the root support of your people— would be to meet your end for sure.

"It would be inviting it to you."

Lam stared silently into the fire. Ch'kara placed her hand on his leg, yet still he said nothing.

"It is your decision, your action, and your life," Terlikk sighed, "And no one will argue your will. You have been through so much— much more than the rest of us, and we cannot possibly understand your mind. But we would very much like you to stay with us." Lam finally looked up at the man. "My niece especially would prefer you here," he smiled.

Lam nodded, countless thoughts swaying his mind one way, then another.

"We are all exhausted," a woman Lam knew as the village seamstress spoke up. "Let's all get some rest, and see how things feel in the morning."

Terlikk took the guard duty, and the others bedded down for the night.

Some time after the others had fallen asleep, Ch'kara crept very close to Lam. Slipping under his animal skin covering with him, she placed one arm and one leg over him. "My uncle was right," she whispered in his ear. "I wish you would stay here. I want you to stay with *me*."

Lam wrapped his arms around her, and she wiggled fully on top of him, spreading her body along his. He found this felt wonderful, both inside and outside of his body. Another sort of electricity began coursing through his system, quite pleasantly.

She rested her head on his chest. "I hear your heart here. It speaks of faraway lands, as well as lands nearer to us." Ch'kara lifted her head and looked into his eyes. He saw that her eyes were moist with tears.

"There *is* a place for us here, Lam," she breathed. "It is what was meant to be— I feel that in *my* heart."

Lam nodded as tears formed in his own eyes.

"Yet," she continued, "I can also see the other line of time…"

"The other line?" he asked.

A tear caught the firelight as it escaped her eye and dropped to his chest. "The line you will choose. The line that will take you from me."

"Ch'kara, Ch'kara," he lifted a hand and stroked her hair. "No, I will come back to you. I will make things right in this place, and return to you to stay from then on!"

She stifled a sob, and shook her head. "No," she said. "No…"

He raised his head and pressed his lips to hers. She returned the kiss with an intensity that sent the electricity in his body to new levels.

"Yes, dear one, I will."

She shook her head and kissed him again, long and hard, without ever taking her eyes from his.

"Yes…" he whispered between the moments of their lips meeting.

Their hands caressed each other's faces. She ran her fingers through his hair as his hands began to explore the curves of her waist and legs. Their lips and tongues explored each other, and their eyes never broke contact. Ch'kara felt the hardness growing between Lam's legs.

When she slipped her hand inside his tunic and touched his chest, shivers of pleasure flooded his body. He instantly slid his fingers inside her own clothing. The small moan that escaped her when he gathered her soft breasts into his hands was like cool water after a hot day in the field. His hardness pressed against her, and she began to slowly move her hips against it.

With their eyes still locked on each other, and their kisses full of hunger and intensity, she quickly reached down and removed him from his clothing. The heat of it sent her body out of control. She eagerly gathered her skirts, and pressed him inside her.

Their intimate moment did not last long, but the sensations of it lingered on their skin through the night as they slept together, arms wrapped tightly around each other as if nothing else mattered.

• FIFTEEN •

When Ch'kara woke, she knew that something else *did* matter.

She watched Lam prepare to journey back toward the land of the Gildok tribe, and fought the urge to weep again. There would be plenty of time for that later.

The others of the remnant had now gathered as well. They encircled Lam as they had done when the Shen-Ma had first sat on him and declared him The Seed. He thought of all that had happened between that time and now, and tears once again appeared in his eyes.

He looked to the sky in the hopes his other people would be above him in this journey, but found the sky clear and blue. There were no clouds to be seen.

Terlikk gave no more lectures or speeches. He merely bowed to Lam, and then embraced him. "This is from your mother," he said. He then embraced him a second time. "And this is from me."

The other nine followed his example, and Lam was weeping openly by the end.

Wiping his eyes, he turned to Ch'kara. She placed

a hand on each side of his face and pulled his head to hers. Forehead to forehead and eye to eye, no words were needed between them. She kissed his lips long and slow before releasing him and stepping back.

Lam looked at them all one by one. "I *will* return," he said. "I am of the stars."

He did not see Terlikk shake his head sadly as he walked into the forest.

The journey back through the trees was full of emotion for Lam. All he had been through, all he had just done, and all he was on his way to do washed over him in waves. But through it all, his mind never wavered from his decision. He had no doubt this was what he was to do.

When he came to his ghost of a village again, he was forced to sit down on a large root. Time passed as he became lost in his flood of thoughts and feelings. He was not aware how long he had been staring at Ric'ua's hut, but he was not able to bring himself to go near it. Lam was glad the others planned to come here in a couple more days, to build a pyre and lay the bodies of their families to rest properly. It should have been done already, but the remnant was allowing time to pass, to make sure the Gildoks believed there were no survivors, in case they came back to check.

Lam saw no sign that the Gildoks had returned to the village. But why had they done this thing in the first place? He simply could not wrap his mind around it. The Shen-Ma had said it was not because of him, but he felt responsible nevertheless. The violent tribe's last visit had been because of him, though that had been nearly a year ago.

It had grown to be late afternoon, and the sun had begun its climb down from the sky. He had no specific plan yet of what he would do to the Gildoks, but he would sneak close and begin by observing. The cover of darkness would provide him the ability to watch and listen undetected. Then he would know what could be done.

Lam stood from the root, scooped up a gurja fruit, and headed toward the Gildok land.

What did he hope to accomplish with this mission? What did he expect to do— wipe them out in return for what they had done to his village? He had no idea how he would do that. It was true he was from the stars, but apart from The Remnant and inside a physical body, what advantage did he truly have? Perhaps, if he was in his energy form, he could zap them from above, but he was not.

He still held the advantage of a broader sense of awareness of what it meant to be alive than the tribes of people in this place had, but even so, wasn't he acting on the same bodily emotions the rest of the people were? Was that then truly any advantage?

He smelled them before he saw them. A pungent mixture of sweat, body waste, and roasting meat swirled around him. Was the nauseous feeling in his belly from the smell, or from the anxiousness of his arrival to their land?

Lam slowed his pace, cautiously avoiding stepping on twigs and leaves. He came up behind a large tree and peeked around it to see their night fires already blazing high. Silhouetted figures moved around the flames, preparing the village for night, much as his own neighbors had done each evening. From this point of view, these violent people seemed… normal. Were there really any differences between these people and his people? What was it that made them so aggressive, and his village so peaceful?

A movement to his left caught his eye. It was a man! Had he been found?

He pressed against the tree and held his breath. The man slowly came to the other side of his tree, and then continued on.

Lam released his breath. It had just been a guard patrolling the edge of the village.

His own village had never set a guard, even after so many attacks from the Gildoks and the Furds. Were these people *so* fearful of losing something that they could not even allow themselves to rest in the night hours?

Lam looked up at the large tree. Perhaps it would not only be safer in a tree, but he would be able to see their routines better from a higher perspective. There were no branches low enough on this tree to climb. He glanced around until he spotted a smaller tree. After checking that the guard was not nearby, he quickly made his way over to it, and scrambled to the top.

He found he *could* see into the village much better from here. A large group of them were gathered around the largest of the three fires burning in their central space. They were listening intently to one figure in particular. Was that their Shen-Ma? Did they even have seers and spirit-talkers? Lam smiled. He was sure they didn't have any walk-ins from distant star systems.

Turning his attention back to the gathering, he saw the one they had been listening to was now standing, and perfectly motionless. The crowd around the one was shuffling and shifting. Squinting into the darkness, Lam saw they, too, were standing to their feet, and were all turning to face the same direction.

His heart skipped in his chest.

Were they facing *him?* Had they somehow spotted him in the tree? He didn't see how— it was a moonless night, and he was well away from any firelight. The tension in his body seemed to lock him in place rather than help him make any quick decisions what to do.

The figure was moving now. The others fell behind the one, following.

And they were definitely heading straight toward Lam.

The figure walked directly and unwaveringly up to the tree Lam was in, and the crowd circled the base of the tree completely. Each and every one of them was looking right at him as he clung to the highest branch that would bear his weight.

Lam saw the lead figure was an old man rather than an old woman, with features so fierce it sent a shudder through his body simply to look at.

"This is he," the old man growled to the others. "This is the one who came onto our sacred lands, and tainted the holy fruits of our labor.

"And yet…" He seemed to be straining to hear something. "And yet he is *not* the one."

The old man's eyes suddenly grew very large. "No!" he gasped. "No! This cannot be! Quickly! Bring the axes! This *was* the one who came to steal our wealth, but he is now the one that has come to steal our very souls! Cut him down! He must not be allowed to escape this time!

"He is not from this place! He has stolen life, and must not be allowed to keep it, or he will steal our souls as well!

"The dreaded prophecy we hoped would be

overturned by all our good works has manifested nevertheless! CUT HIM DOWN!"

A familiar jolt shot through Lam's body as the first axe struck the base of the tree.

His thoughts immediately went to Ch'kara. He knew at once she had been right, and he simultaneously wished he was with her right now. Why had he left? Why hadn't even the promise of love been enough to persuade him to not continue with this dangerous mission of anger and pain?

The vibrations came to a halt, and a slow creaking sound grew into a loud cracking sound.

"Ready yourselves!" the old man cried as the tree began to tilt. "The devil is coming down!"

With a final snap, the tree began to plummet to the earth, but Lam found he remained suspended in the air. He watched himself tumble to the ground with a crash. The crowd roared as they rushed toward him.

There it goes.

Lam turned to The Remnant beside him.

I've lost everything now.

You've lost your body now.

I've lost our hope.

You still bear the mind of the lower vibration. You have gained everything again.

But I've lost my body. I've lost my self. I've lost us.

You never lost us.

We are The Remnant.

You have carried us with you always.

You have planted the seed.

You have secured the knowledge of our people.

It will grow.

It will remember.

It will carry us on.

But we ourselves…
You still bear the mind of the lower vibration.
We are not bodies.
We do not depend on bodies.
We are not attached.

But I've lost even our chance of salvation! I've dissolved us all!

We will *join the dissolution. We will not be ended.*
Our memory continues among the society below.
We will not be lost.
Look at your body, Lam.

He returned his focus to the scene below. He watched in amazement as his body jumped up and ran into the darkness of the forest, the angry mob in close pursuit.

What will happen to it?
It no longer matters.
Two societies have now been joined.
Two societies have now been saved.
The seed has been planted.
The root has been laid.

• EPILOGUE •

With a final strain and a piercing cry, she shoved with all her might.

Another cry was immediately heard— small, yet clearly strong. An audible gasp of breath was followed by yet another cry.

She let her head fall to the earth. She watched the immense cloud that had sheltered her labor from the harshness of the sun begin to dissipate as her breathing began to slow and return to normal. Laughter bubbled from deep inside her. Her tears of pain became tears of pure joy as she listened to the most wonderful sounds she had ever heard.

Nearly nine moons had passed since he had left, yet she seemed to feel him closer beside her now more than ever before. She had known before he ever left he would never return, that she would never lay eyes on him again.

But that was all right.

The spirits with her and within her that had shown her these things had also kept her company, just as his own energy had. To some aspects of herself, it was as if he had never left her at all.

And now she knew she would feel these things even more intensely.

She smiled as she stretched out her arms to receive the bundle now being delivered to her.

"Beloved Shen-Ma," Terlikk said, "Ch'kara.

"Behold, your daughter."

— • —

He who has gone,
so we but cherish his memory,
abides with us
more potent, nay, more present
than the living man.

Antoine de Saint-Exupéry

— • —

• ABOUT THE AUTHOR •

Lloyd Matthew Thompson was raised in a very strict religious household, the oldest of nine children. He has since explored, experienced, and been shaped by many other pathways, including Buddhism, Shamanism, Paganism, and New Age. Whether writing, painting, drawing or teaching, reflections of all these can be found in his work.

He has written for various metaphysical and holistic blogs and magazines, both locally and globally. He is the author of *The Healer: A Novel,* as well as the nonfiction books *The Galaxy Healer's Guide* and *Lightworker: A Call to Authenticity.*

Lloyd currently lives in Oklahoma City, Oklahoma, with his wife, triplets, daughter who thinks she is a cat, and cat who thinks she is a daughter.

More information on all his work can be found at **www.StarfieldPress.com**

ALSO BY LLOYD MATTHEW THOMPSON

THE ENERGY OF GOD

WISE ONE: THE SONG OF MANJUSHRI

LIGHTWORKER: A CALL TO AUTHENTICITY

ENERGYWORKER: A CALL TO EMPOWERMENT

THE HEALER: A Novel

ROOT: A Novella

AURA: A Short Story

GOOD NIGHT, NURSE

THE
ENERGY
OF
GOD

*In the beginning
was the Love...*

LLOYD MATTHEW THOMPSON
BESTSELLING AUTHOR OF *LIGHTWORKER: A CALL TO AUTHENTICITY*

THE HEALER

A NOVEL

LLOYD MATTHEW THOMPSON

www.ingramcontent.com/pod-product-compliance
Lightning Source LLC
Chambersburg PA
CBHW070638130626

46555CB00006B/2595